Roses Are Red & His Thug Love is True:

Aaliyah x Jahiem

Written By: Jamie Marie

Want to be a part of Kellz K Publishing?

To submit your manuscript to Kellz K Publishing, please end the first three chapters & synopsis to

kellzkpublishing@gmail.com

"My baby gone Jaheim, somebody done took my baby from me."

"Don't tell me that, auntie. I drove as fast as I could to get here. He ain't gone. Tell me he ain't gone."

"My baby is gone, Jah. I don't know how I'm gone make the through this."

"I 'm gone find the motherfuckers who did this, and on my mama, they gone fucking pay for this shit."

"Snoop, find that bitch who was with Kelton. Find that hoe tonight, and I want the niggas that killed my cousin. I don't give a fuck where they are or who they're with. I want they fucking location tonight. I got a feeling this bitch set him up, and a bitch gone talk when they scared. Once I get her to talk, she's fucking dead."

I left the hospital with murder on my mind. If only Kel would have just come on the block with me, he would be here right now. I couldn't believe this shit. I really didn't have shit to live for. Both of my parents were gone, my bitch fucked up on me, and now my best friend/ my brother was dead. My heart was already cold, but now that shit was dead. Fuck love! Fuck everything! Them motherfuckers were going to pay. If it took the rest of my life, they were gone fucking pay. If them niggas thought I was ruthless now, they had no idea what I was capable of. Anybody could feel me, and I wasn't stopping until I turned this city red for Kelton, and that was on both my dead parents.

***

That night I sat in my car just lurking for anything or anybody who knew anything about Kelton's murder. The way that Hennessey had me feeling, my trigger finger was itching. The fucking streets weren't talking, and the shit was pissing me off. I called Snoop and let him know that as soon as he heard anything to hit my line. I don't give a fuck what it was. Niggas were paying and with their life. I went to the crib and cried through the fucking pain. I was tired of losing niggas to the streets. Kelton would be the last loss that I took to the fucking streets. Once I found his killers, I was done. It was time to let this street shit go. I don't think I could take any more L's.

Two Years Later

Aaliyah

"**D**amn Chantell, look at this picture this nigga just posted. Damn, this nigga is fine."

"Girl, just go talk to that man cause I am tired of hearing about his ass every damn day."

Every time this nigga come through the hood, I was staring at him. Jaheim was the shit, and he knew it. Here it was one month before Valentine's Day, and like every other year, I didn't have a date or anything planned. Usually, I would just watch Netflix and binge watch until Netflix was watching me. I wanted different for this year. This year I wanted Jaheim. Jaheim was the sexiest dude in the hood I had ever laid my eyes on. From the way that he kept his dreads neatly twisted to the way, he wore his jeans. When he smiled, he had the whitest, perfect teeth that I have ever seen. The gold fronts he would sometimes wear would drive any female crazy.

Jaheim stood about 6'2 and was good and solid at 300 pounds. He definitely towered over me. I only stood 4'11. It was cold in the south, so it was definitely big boy season, and a bitch like me was always cold. I wasn't a bad looking female, but I wasn't the baddest bitch around either. Most would call me the shy type of female. I was a bigger woman, but I had learned to love my curves. I worked hard at toning up. I had my own style, and I loved it. I knew how to dress sexy and keep it classy. I worked at Bath and Body Works, and I went to the local community college studying to be a health care worker and an advocate for underprivileged children. Children were my passion, and I prayed to one day have a big family, at least four kids.

"Man, Aaliyah, stop stalking that nigga and come with me to this card game and party tonight. You know I hate being around Demario and his cousin."

"Then why are you going, Chantelle?"

"Cause I wanna be with my man duh, plus all them ugly bitches gone be over there, and I need to keep an eye on my man. I can't have them ugly bitches trying to get all on him the fuck. I have spent too much time building that man up for me to have another bitch come in, hell no."

"Girl, you know Demario is too fucking scared of your ass to even look at another female the wrong way."

"And it better stay that way, or else his ass gone get what the fuck he got last time, but fucking worst. I am not fucking with Demario's ass."

I didn't know what kind of relationship Chantelle and Demario had. They were high school sweethearts and each other's first everything. Demario cheated on Chantelle one time, and she went off on the both of them. After she knocked the girl completely out, she not only took a bat and broke all of his and her car windows, but she flattened their tires and proceeded to beat Demario with the bat. The poor boy suffered two cracked ribs and a broken elbow. Chantelle spent two nights in jail, but neither one of them pressed charges, so she was free to go. I told Chantelle that she should have left his dumb ass that time, but she didn't listen.

Chantelle was beautiful. I'm talking Model Naomi Campbell beautiful and could have any man she wanted, but she was sticking it out with Demario. From that day on, Mario was like a little puppy following Chantelle around. I understand she was hurt, but I would have just let his cheating ass go, but she was in love with him. Like the old saying goes *"what's understood, didn't need to be explained."*

I really didn't like being around his people either. They were a bunch of potheads and ratchet ass females who loved drama, but I didn't have anything else planned so might as well go. Card games in the south were a big deal. Whether spades, pity pat, or gin rummy, whatever our card games got serious, especially when money was involved. I was a big spades player a few years ago. My mother and I would do some damage on a spades table. Since her passing, I haven't been able to find the perfect partner and Chantelle was helpless.

"I guess I will go out there, Chantelle. I ain't doing shit else, but I'm riding with you. I'm not driving my shit to the west side. Niggas won't fuck my shit up."

"Aight Aaliyah, just be ready by ten, please."

"I will be."

"Ok Aaliyah, I will be back at ten tonight."

***

It was only 5:30, so I had plenty of time to relax before tonight. I decide to go to the mall and have myself a little retail therapy session. I wanted to hit a few of my favorite stores. It was wintertime in the south, so I needed a few more scarfs and some new boots. For a big girl, I had my own style. I loved colors and patterns. I loved pairing different patterns and colors together to make it my on. I wasn't very tall only standing 4'11, so heels were my best friend. I loved a nice pair of sexy heels, especially boots.

I had to hit up my favorite store first which was Lane Bryant. Victoria Secret was out of the question for me when it came to bras and panties. I was lucky if I could fit one titty or even one thigh in anything from Victoria Secret. They had some cute sets but nothing for me. I found a few sets and headed to my next stop, JC Penney. I saw these sexy ass, black, thigh high boots online, and I was hoping that they had them in the store cause I really wanted to wear them before it got warm outside, and just my luck, they had them and in my size.

I walked the mall for a while. I admired some of the couples and their children in the mall. I was a sucker for family, but I had to find a man first. I had relationships in the past, but nothing serious. My last relationship with Brandon was fun until I realized how much of a dog he was and played the fuck out of me. I would give this nigga money just for him to buy the next bitch some food. The fuck kind of shit was that, but I was blind to that shit for almost two years. When I ended things with Brandon, I promised I would never let another nigga play me, and I meant that on everything. After Brandon, I developed a severe case of depression. Brandon would use my weight to make me feel bad about myself. After we broke up, with Brandon, I was a victim of body shaming.

I left the mall around eight o'clock, and I decided to go home and take my time getting dressed. There was no need to rush. We were not leaving until ten. I wanted to wear something cute tonight, but not too fancy. I decided on a cute black and gray sweater dress that would go perfectly with my new boots and one of the scarfs that I bought today. I had a bomb ass playlist that I got from Alishia one of my homegirls from work. She knew how to make a bomb ass 80s and 90's R&B playlist, which was just what I needed it. I poured myself a glass of wine and turned the music up to the perfect volume. I grabbed my favorite lotion and bubble bath.

***

At about 9:45, I was fully dressed and almost ready. I just needed to put some lip gloss on my lips and to lay my edges down. I had just gotten my back and sides cleaned up at the barbershop, so I was good. I kept a short haircut, so there wasn't much to do to my hair. I had to admit that the dress was hugging every curve I had. I was proud of my shape and my curves. I could definitely keep a nigga warm during the winter. I snapped a quick selfie and posted on all of my social media accounts with the caption, *"Every curve is perfectly placed"*.

At ten o'clock exactly, Chantelle was outside blowing her horn like a straight fool. I grabbed my keys, phone, and left my house. I made sure all doors and windows were locked, I didn't trust these little badass kids around my apartment.

"Why the hell are you blowing your horn like that, Chantelle?"

"Because Demario left to go to the party before me, and I told him I would be there at ten exactly. I don't trust them bitches on the west side. I don't wanna have to fuck somebody up tonight."

"Chantelle, if you're going to this party to turn up and act a fool, I will stay the fuck home."

"Ain't nothing gone happen, Aaliyah, stop being so damn scary."

"It ain't about being scary. It's about me not bailing your ass out of jail."

"Aaliyah, come on. Let's just go nothing gone happen."

I heard Chantelle say nothing would happen, but I had a bad feeling about tonight I couldn't put my finger on it, but I felt like something was gonna happen. I tried to shake the feeling. By the time we made it to where the party was on the west side, the house and the yard were already packed, and the scent of weed was so strong that you could get a contact high just by breathing in the air. I saw a few people from the mall that worked at random stores and a few from school, but nobody I really fucked with like that. As soon as we walked in the house, Chantelle spotted Demario and practically ran over there two him and sat right on his lap. I just shook my head, walked over to where they were, and took a seat.

***

We were there for about two hours and surprisingly shit was going smooth. The music was bumping, the food was good as hell, and I had a few drinks. I even jumped on the pity pat table and won about two hundred dollars, which was pretty damn good for me.

"Aaliyah, come ride to the store with me. I need to go get Demario some more blunts."

"Why he can't go? If I leave, I am going home. I have to work tomorrow."

"Aaliyah, come on. Let me go get his shit then I will take you home."

"Damn Chantelle, come on man.

Although the ride to the store was only a 10-minute drive there and back, I was ready to go home, get in my bed, and sleep until it was time for me to get ready for work tomorrow.

"I'm gone run this to Demario, and I will be right back to take you home."

"Ok, just don't be forever, Chantelle."

I sat in the car scrolling through my Facebook timeline, looking to see if Jaheim has posted any more pictures or had posted his location. Just my luck his sexy ass posted a picture about 20 minutes ago, and his location said he was on the west side. I wondered where he could be on this side. About five minutes later, I heard a whole bunch of noise sounding like someone was fighting. I got out of the car to see what was going on, and my instinct was right. Chantelle was beating the hell out of some girl. I didn't know who the fuck ole girl was, but the bitch was practically naked. I didn't know what the fuck was going on. I looked around to the see if I could spot Demario to help me stop Chantelle, but this nigga was laid out on the floor with a big ass gash on his forehead, with pieces of a broken glass vase scattered beside him. *I just know this dumb nigga ain't get caught fucking that girl.*

I ran over to where Chantelle and the girl were fighting to try to stop Chantelle before the cops came.

"Chantelle girl, stop. Calm down. What the fuck is going on?"

"Fuck Demario! I come back, and this bitch is on her knees sucking his dick while his bitch ass is laid the fuck back smoking a fucking blunt. Fuck this bitch and his stupid ass!"

"Chantelle, come on. Let's get out of here before someone calls the cops."

"Nah fuck that, I'll go to fucking jail. On my mama, I want Demario's ass dead. His bitch ass is out here making me look stupid. Let me the fuck go, Liyah!"

I couldn't hold Chantelle any longer, that girl was like a damn bull when she was mad. She broke loose from my hold and dove right back on top of ole girl. Demario's dumb ass was still laid out on the floor. I ran back to try and get Chantelle before she killed that girl, but as I was running, I felt two huge hands grab me and pick me up. I snatched around ready to knock a bitch out for having the nerve to grab me, and I locked eyes with Jaheim. He was wearing the same exact outfit from his Facebook post. *Damn, he looked even better up close and personal and smelled so damn good.* The way I was feeling at that moment, I could just snatch my dress over my head and bend down over the table.

"Yo, get your friend. That's my little cousin she's over there fighting."

"I was going to get her until you stopped me, and your little cousin deserves to get her ass beat if she is sucking another woman's man dick and in public at that. Now, if you would excuse me."

I eased past Jaheim and ran over to Chantelle. I managed to get a good tight grip on her and got her off of the girl. Jaheim and some other dude ran over, snatched the chick up, and took her to the back. Although I had a good grip on Chantelle, she was still swinging and trying to break free.

"Chantelle, on God and my mama, if you hit me I'm gone knock your ass the fuck out!" I hated to yell and threaten Chantell, but the way she was swinging, she came close to hitting me twice.

I was finally able to get her in the car and somewhat calmed down. I turned around to head to the driver's side of the car and ran smacked dab into Jaheim again.

"Excuse me," I whispered lowly to Jaheim. Damn, he was so intimidating.

"It's cool. I didn't mean to scare you. I was just coming over to apologize for going off in the house. I didn't know what was going on. I just saw my little cousin getting her ass beat and jumped into protective big cousin mode."

"It's cool, I understand."

"You good, did you get your homegirl to calm down?"

"Yeah, for now, I had to threaten to slap her tho?"

"Damn, she's pissed."

"Nah, not pissed more hurt than anything, I gotta go take her home and make sure she's good, I already know this gone be a very long night."

"Aight, Aaliyah, I will see you around."

"Wait, how do you know my name?"

"I know a lot, later."

I walked around to the driver's side of the car with the biggest, goofiest smile on my face. My biggest thought was how did he know my name, and what did he mean by he knows a lot? This would surely be on my mind all night, but right now, I had to deal with my best friend.

Jaheim

"No, fuck that, Regina. I ain't finding no damn body. You brought this on yourself. We all done told you about messing with everybody's man."

"What you mean, Jah? He stepped to me, shit. I just said yes."

"And that's why you got your ass beat last night. You knew that man had a girl. Hell, she's been sitting in his lap all damn night, and as soon as she leaves, here you go switching over there to him."

"Shit, he called me over there, Jah. What I was supposed to turn him down?"

"Regina, you sound real fucking dumb right now, I am not even going to entertain your dumb ass anymore. I'm out cause you sound real fucking stupid."

"So Jah, you're not gone help me find that bitch who fucked my face up?"

I straight walked out of the house on Regina's dumb ass. I couldn't stand to be in the same room with her ass anymore. The more she talked, the more she pissed me off. I had some of the most ratchet cousins ever, but they were family. My Aunt Sarah asked me to watch after them when their brother got murder two years back. That was a big shock to our family. My aunt hasn't been the same since then, and the girls have gotten out of hand. I have tried to do everything I could, but I honestly just felt like giving up. The only thing that kept me here was that my aunt was like a second mother to me. She took me in when both of my parents were killed in a car accident when I was seven. My aunt has always been there for me, so when her oldest child Kelton got shot and killed, I knew I had to step up.

Kelton and I were like brothers. When he was killed that took a lot out of me. For so long I was just angry and wanted revenge, but of course, the streets weren't talking, so I just focused on getting my money up and building my business, but trust me when I say I promised myself that whoever capped my cousin was going to pay. Just because I wasn't heavy in the streets anymore didn't mean shit. I was still that nigga who could bring niggas to their knees for disrespecting me. The city was still talking about me and the shit I did. I hustled in these streets but I hustled to survive. I wasn't trying to run the streets forever.

Right now, I was focusing on opening my second shop. I was the owner and operator of Detailed LLC. It was a local car detail shop. I did it all in my shop— tint, rims, customs paint jobs— whatever you needed, I could do. I was a beast with my hands. I could hook any car up. That was my passion. Right now, I was headed to my main shop to interview some people for the management position for my new store. I needed another storefront because one location wasn't enough. I had people coming from all over the state for me and my crew to hook their rides up.

I left my aunt's house with a headache after talking to Regina. She deserved to get her ass beat messing with that nigga. Sucking dick or not, he still had a girl. I decided to take the long way to the shop. I had a few minutes to kill before the interviews started. I just wanted to ride and clear my head for a few. I made it to my shop around 1:30 and interviews were starting at 2:00 o'clock.

I walked into the building and saw my store receptionist Cherie doing everything but work of course. Cherie was another one of my cousins, she was my Aunt Sarah's middle child, and she was just as bad if not worse than Regina. The only reason she still had a job was because she had a daughter that she had to support. Had it not been for her daughter Arianna, I would have fired her ratchet ass long ago.

"Cherie, why is your front desk such a mess. You gotta keep this place clean. First impressions are very important. Clean this mess up. You know we got interviews today."

"Well, hello to you too, cousin. You came in here bitching and couldn't even speak."

"Cherie, just get it done, please. I will be in my office getting things ready for the interviews."

I had about four interviews set up for today. Each candidate was able to pass the assessment, the phone interview, and the personality test. I know that sounds like a lot, but I needed the right person to run my store.

***

At about 3:45, I was finished with my interviews, and I had my two finalists, Stacy and Erica. Stacy seemed more professional as far as appearance and job performance. On the other hand, Erica seemed more business-minded she had a lot of ideas to improve business and gain more exposure to the company. This was going to be a tough decision. I sat back in my chair and thought about this decision. I had to make the right choice. This second shop was going to put my business even further on the map.

Aaliyah

"Chantelle, I am headed to work honey. Do you need anything before I go?"

"No Liyah, I'm good."

"Chantelle it has been two days, and you have not left my house or my couch, for that matter. Look, I know you're hurting, but this should only make you stronger and know your worth. Demario's lying ass didn't respect you, cause if he did, that shit would have never happened, and I hope you done with his ass for good now."

"Aaliyah, I love that man with everything, and he just continues to hurt me, but I need him so bad."

"You know what, Chantelle? I am not going to entertain this conversation any longer. If you happen to leave, make sure you lock up my house, please. See you later girl."

I walked outside and headed to work. I didn't understand her logic how could you need a man that constantly hurts you and puts you through shit. It just didn't make any sense to me, but maybe I was never truly in love, but if love made you need a night that dogged you out then I was good, I didn't want it.

I made it to work at about 8:50 a.m. I was working the 9 to 5:30 shift today. We were currently in the middle of our huge semi-annual and Valentine's sale at Bath and Body works, so the line was already forming by the time I arrived. I already knew that today was going to be hectic, but I honestly enjoyed the rush of it. I was still on winter break from my classes, so I picked up a few extra hours during the week just to pass the time.

***

It was now one o'clock, and I was beyond ready for my lunch break. I needed the entire hour to myself. I walked outside to my car.

"What the fuck! Who the fuck hit my car?"

Some idiot had clearly backed into my shit, busted my light, and scratched my shit up. My car was black so whoever hit my shit drove a red car.

"The fuck, man?" They then had the nerve to leave a damn sorry note. What type of shit is that?

I had lost my damn appetite. I now had to spend my lunch break looking for a good and reliable detail shop to get my shit fixed. I took to Facebook looking for recommendations. Within minutes of posting my status, I had about seven places to consider. The most popular was this place called Bossed Up over on the north side, and this placed called Detailed LLC. My job was closer to the shop on the north side, so I decided to go by there when I got off.

***

I got out the car still mad as fuck about my car. I decided to cut my lunch break short and just take 30 minutes so that I could leave early to have my car looked at. It was 4:30, and I was out of there. I put the location of the shop in the GPS app on my iPhone XR and let Siri guide me to my destination. Arriving I saw a sign on the door that said they were closed, which pissed me off even more because their Facebook page said they were opened until seven o'clock. Mad as hell I put the other destination in and drove the nearly 15-minute drive to the shop. Thankfully this shop was still opened, so hopefully, I could get my car looked at.

Walking into the shop, the interior was nicely decorated the sounds of "Cupid" by 112 played softly through the surround sound. There wasn't anyone at the front desk. However, there was a bell, so I rang the bell and waited. About two minutes later, a female, who I assume was the desk clerk, came from the back. I could tell she had an attitude by the way she popped her gum and looked me up and down. I felt a little offended by the way she looked be up and down, but I kept my comments to myself... for now.

"May I help you?" The attitude on this broad was too much, and she really needed to pipe that shit down before she got snatched across the counter.

"Yes, I need someone to look at my car. Someone backed into me at work, broke my tail light, and scratched my car leaving red paint on the back."

"If you got insurance, fill this paper out with all of your information."

"Ok thank you."

I looked over the paperwork and filled out everything that was needed and took it back up to that rude ass girl. After a five minute wait, I heard my name called to come to the back, and I could have sworn I heard that voice before. I grabbed my bag and headed to the back.

"Ms. James?"

"Jaheim, you work here?"

"Nah, Aliyah I own this. This is my shop."

"Oh, my bad, congratulations."

"Thanks, so I see from your paperwork that someone backed into you, busted your tail light, and also left scratching and paint from their car, is that it?"

"Yeah, that's pretty much it."

"Ok well, let's go outside and take a look."

I followed Jaheim outside to my car so that he could look at my damages. How could I not have known that this was his shop? As much as I stalk his social media accounts, I should know everything about him down to his shoe size. Watching him move around my car had me getting really hot and bothered. The way he looked so focused on the damages to the way he wrote on his clipboard. The things I imagined doing to this man were definitely Pornhub worthy. I wanted this man in the worst way.

"Aaliyah, did you hear me?" Jaheim's deep baritone voice startled me out of my sexual fantasy.

"Huh, no. What did you say?"

"I asked you if you could bring your car back in the morning so that I could get started on it?"

"Yeah, I have to be at work at 10:30 so is around 10 o'clock good? I'll just let Chantelle follow me to drop it off."

"Aight, bet and how is your friend anyway?"

"Still at my house crying every hour getting on my nerves about that fuck nigga."

"Like you said, she's hurt right she just needs some time."

"Yeah, I guess. I will be glad when she realizes that Demario is a fucking dog and will never change."

"Well, you just got to let her learn on her own, but just be that shoulder she needs."

The way this man spoke was fucking amazing I didn't think it was possible for anyone to even form their words so perfectly, but that's exactly what he was doing. I could stand here and listen to him talk for hours.

"I am there for her as best as I can, but I can be back up here tomorrow morning. Do you know how long it will take?"

"What time do you get off?"

"Six o'clock.

"Then your car will be ready at six o'clock."

After a few minutes of staring at Jaheim, I was able to make my way to my car and drive home. I put on my Trey Songz playlist and allowed Trigga's voice to guide me home. As "Jupiter Love" played through my car, I fantasized about Jaheim. I made it home and noticed that Chantelle was still there. I didn't mind at all that my best friend stayed with me. She needed me at this time, and I would be there without a doubt, but I hated to see her hurting like this over that dog ass Demario.

I grabbed my things and made my way in the house, I didn't see Chantelle at first, but as I walked closer to the bathroom, and I heard "On Bended Knee" by Boyz II Men playing. I could hear soft sniffles coming from the bathroom, which confirmed that Chantelle was crying. I gently knocked on the door and turned the knob to let myself in. Chantelle was seating on the floor with her phone in her hand crying. My heart truly broke for my best friend. She was hurting, and I was being insensitive. I took my shoes off, got down on the floor with Chantelle, and held her while she cried. Chantelle cried for about 10 minutes until she finally spoke.

"Why would he continue to hurt me, Liyah? I did everything for him, and I just found out that he has been with that bitch before. Apparently they've been messaging each other through Facebook."

"How do you know that?"

"I have had the password and login to all of Demario's social media accounts for a while, but he never gave me a reason to use them until now. They've been fucking behind my back for a while, but here is the worst part. She ain't the only one. It's about five bitches he's been entertaining right up under my nose, and I didn't even suspect anything."

"I truly hate that nigga, Chantelle. It's time for you to leave his ass alone because now he is putting you in a world of danger by fucking different bitches like that.

"Aaliyah, I am done with his ass for good. He can beg and plead all he wants, but we are done. I just blocked his number and him on social media, and I hope I did some damage when I knocked his ass out with that vase, stupid motherfucker."

"You know I got your back every step of the way, so whatever you want, I got you boo. Tell you what, let's go get some food and drinks and enjoy our night?"

"Ok let's go."

We both got up and went our separate ways to get ourselves together. Times like this I was thankful to have two bathrooms because we both took out sweet times getting ready. I opted to wear something simple I chose a pair of black distressed jeans and a cream-colored Polo sweater with my tan Timberlands on my feet. I put a few curls in my hair, a little eyeliner and lip gloss, and I was ready. Chantelle looked cute in her Champion sweat suit and black Air Max on her feet.

We decided to go to California Dreaming and just enjoy good food and drinks. Thankfully, the restaurant was not as crowded as it usually is, so our wait time to be seated was only five minutes. I ordered the bacon wrapped chicken with grilled baby corn and loaded mashed potatoes, while Chantelle feasted on a huge T-bone steak with sautéed greens and rice. I for one didn't know how people could eat steak. It tasted like rubber to me but to each its own.

***

We ate and enjoyed drinks for about three hours, I didn't drink as much as Chantelle because I was the driver, but I did enjoy two tequila sunrises, anyone who knows me knows that Patrón is my drink of choice, and I can drink a bottle in one night. We left around midnight and headed home. Chantelle was done. She was asleep before we left the parking lot. We made it home, and I managed to get

Chantelle's drunk ass in the house and in the bed. I said a quick prayer over my best friend.

I made it to my room stripped down to my bra and panties and got into my bed. Checking my phone, I had some Facebook and Instagram notifications along with an inbox message. I was shocked to see that the request and inbox were from Jaheim. I accept his friend request, and there were a few hearts on a few of my most recent pictures. I opened the inbox, and my heart was beating out of my chest as I read his words

Jaheim Martin: I am looking forward to seeing you tomorrow, after I finish your car, would you have dinner with me?

I could not believe what I was seeing on my phone/ I wanted to scream and jump up and down, but I didn't want to risk waking up Chantelle I saw that he was online, so I decided to message him back;

Aaliyah James: I would love to have dinner with you. What made you decide to ask me out?

Jaheim Martin: I have always had my eyes on you, but I didn't think you were interested. Every time I came through your

hood, you would shy away, but I peeped the way you were watching me earlier today at my shop and decided to shoot my shot.

Aaliyah James: Well, I am glad you decided to shoot your shot, I would never have the nerve to step to you.

Jaheim Martin: Never be afraid lil mama, I'm harmless, but go ahead and get some rest, I will see you in the morning. Good night, Aaliyah.

Aaliyah James: Good night, Jaheim.

I could not believe my eyes. Not only was I talking to Jaheim Martin, but he also asked me on a date. I read over the messages about five times before placing my phone on the charger and going to sleep. Tomorrow was going to be a great day.

Jaheim

I swear mornings came quickly. It was as if I just went to sleep an hour ago, and it was time to get back up. Here it was eight o'clock, and I was tired as fuck, but money had to be made. I said my morning prayer and answered a few emails for work and a few text messages from a few females I fucked with from time to time but nothing serious. I opened my Facebook messenger and sent lil mama a good morning message. It was something about her that caught my eye, and with the way she watched me yesterday, I knew she was feeling me.

I have seen Aaliyah around the way for a while, and of course, I asked questions about her. I wanted to know if she had a man before I stepped to her. Aaliyah was not only beautiful, but she was thick in all the right places. She had a natural beauty, so she didn't always have her face caked with makeup. I was the type of nigga who wanted to see the same face at night and in the morning. All that makeup, I couldn't get with all that. I usually liked my women with long hair so I would have something to pull on when I'm beating that pussy from the back, but Aaliyah was sexy with her short haircut. That shit fit her perfectly. I saw that lil mama messaged me back, but I took a few minutes before I responded. I took that time to go in the bathroom to complete my morning hygiene and get ready to start my day.

Aaliyah James: Good morning Jaheim, I hope you slept well,

Jaheim Martin: I did sleep well after talking to you.

Aaliyah James: You got me blushing.

Jaheim Martin: Well then, I am doing something right, but let me get dressed I will see you @10.

Aaliyah James: Ok I will be there.

I locked my phone and headed to the shower. Thoughts of Aaliyah had my dick rocking up. Those hips and those curves were perfectly positioned. As I said, she was thick in all the right places. Visions of me in between those thick thighs had me stroking my dick in the shower. I released my seeds and continued my shower.

About an hour later, I was headed out the door and on my way to work, I only lived 10 minutes from my main shop, so I was good on time. I wanted to make sure I was there when Aaliyah arrived. I saw that both of my cousins were at the shop and being loud as ever.

I swear these two were starting to piss me off. Just being in their presence had me wanting to knock they asses out.

"Cherie, Regina, why is it so loud in here, and Regina why are you here?"

"Damn Jah, I can't come see my sister at her job?"

"No, because this is a place of business, not your personal gossip area, so hurry cause Cherie has a busy day today."

"Yes sir, boss," I heard Cherie say, but I ignored her ignorance. Pretty soon I would be looking for a front desk clerk and manager for this store. Fuck with me, and I would get Erica for one store, and Stacey for the other. I might just do that.

I walked to the back to get my workday started. I wanted to work on Aaliyah's car personally. I would have my crew get started on the other four cars we had today. My crew consisted of the baddest mechanics and detailed workers ever. They weren't just niggas that I knew from the hood. They were educated and highly skilled workers. Brandon was that nigga who could hook any car up system up and tint the hell out some windows. Keith could just listen to a car and tell you what's wrong with it. Those two were my right and left hand. I trusted them with my shop.

"Good morning, Brandon. How you doing?" I dapped Brandon up as I spoke to him

"Yo, what's up Jah? I'm good you know, just ready to get some work done."

"I feel you, my nigga. We got about four cars today, but one that I want to handle personally."

"Ok, why is that?"

"You know just a pretty little lady that I'm trying to take to dinner."

"Ok Jah, I see you trying to be Rico Suave and shit."

"It ain't nothing like that. I've been peeping shorty for a minute now. The opportunity presented itself and stepped to her."

"I feel you. Do you, Jah. I'm gone head on to the back and get shit set up." I dapped Brandon up again and headed to my office to put my things up and get ready to start my day.

I turned on my computer, and the first thing I saw was the reminder for the management position for the second location. I had to make my decision soon. I was seriously considering letting Cherie go and hiring each of the candidates for each store. I had to sleep on that. I didn't want to disappoint my aunt, but Cherie was useless and causing nothing but havoc.

I sat at my desk deep in thought until I heard Cherie yell my name, I glanced at my computer, and the time read *10:02*, so I figured that must have been lil mama bringing her car. I locked up my office and walked to the front where Cherie had the desk looking like a windstorm came through it, thankfully I had Aaliyah's file in my hand.

"Good morning, Aaliyah."

"Good morning, Jaheim. I didn't know where you wanted me to park my car."

"It's cool. I will move it around to the back."

I looked at Cherie and gave her a look that told her to get her shit together. I then placed my hand on the small of Aaliyah's back and led her outside. I saw that her homegirl that fought with Regina was the one that followed her here, and I prayed nothing popped off at my shop.

"You look nice you sure you're going just to work?" I asked Aaliyah. I saw that beautiful smile and wanted to make sure that smile stayed on her face daily.

"Yes I am headed to work, and I need to get going because I am running a little late."

"Ok I won't hold you up, but remember your car will be finished at six, so does that mean you can meet me for dinner at nine?"

"Umm sure, nine is perfect,"

"Bet I will see you at six and looking forward to nine."

I watched as Aaliyah walk off to her homegirl's car and drive off. I was looking forward to tonight and getting to know lil mama. I haven't been serious about a woman since my last relationship about four years ago with my ex Shanae'. Shanae' and I had a real nasty break up, and after that, I was on my fuck bitches mode. I looked at every female the same, and they were all grimy as fuck. I was taking a chance with lil mama. I just prayed shit didn't backfire on my ass.

I drove Aaliyah's car to the back and got started on it. The car really wasn't that bad, so it didn't take me any time to replace the back light, and the paint touch-up. There was one dent on the back bumper, but that was nothing to fix.

***

I finished Aaliyah's car around 4:30 and drove it back around front. I went ahead, washed it, and cleaned the inside for her, and after that, her car was as good as new. I passed the time by helping the fellas with the other cars they had to finish, which with the three of us were able to knock everything out on one day.

"Damn that tint is dark, Brandon. That's got to be illegal tint."

"Nope, it's just above the legal range for tint. Anybody could see just enough inside to not see anything."

"That shit is hard as fuck tho."

"Who is that pulling up, are you expecting any more clients today, Jah?"

"Nah, that's shawty with the black Mazda I did earlier today. I'm taking lil mama to dinner tonight."

"Oh, word?"

I watched as Aaliyah got out of the car and walked over to me. The smile on her face faded when she saw me talking to Brandon. She had the meanest look on her face by the time she got to me.

"Damn, lil mama, you not happy to see me?"

"Yeah, I'm happy to see you. I just didn't know you had fuck boys working for you."

"Fuck you Aaliyah, you fat ass bitch!"

"Nah Brandon, you never could. Is my car ready?"

The attitude on lil mama was foul. I didn't know what the fuck that exchange they had was all about, but I needed to get to the bottom of this.

"Yeah, your car is ready. Walk with me to the back so that I can get your keys and your receipt."

Walking to the back, I wasn't sure how to approach the situation, I didn't want to come off like I was already her man by questioning her about another nigga, but I damn sure wanted to know what that was about.

"Thank you for fixing my car, Jaheim."

"No thanks needed Aaliyah, but what you and my mans got going on?"

"Brandon is my ex. Brandon dogged the hell out of me for two years, basically played me and made me look like a fool. When I finally found out, he basically said he used me, and I was too fat for him and all types of dumb shit."

"Oh damn, that's fucked up, I wasn't trying to pry or no shit like that. I just wanted to know what all the hostility is all about."

"It's ok. Brandon is a fuck boy, and every time I see him, I remind his dumb ass of that."

"I hope Brandon and I working together doesn't get in the way of me and you and our dinner date."

"Of course not, fuck Brandon. He ruined two years of my life, but he won't get the pleasure of doing that ever again."

"Good, so tonight, where would you like to go? Your choice."

"How about Capital City Grill in the city?"

"Perfect, nine o'clock it is. You got my card just text me your address real quick." I watched as Aaliyah pulled out her iPhone from her back pocket and texted me her address and placed her phone back in her pocket.

"Cool, I got it. I know exactly where you stay. I will be there, come on and check out your car."

I watched as Aaliyah looked at her car and smiled at the work that I have done. She looked pleased, which let me know that I did what she wanted and more.

"Thank you so much. She looked as good as new. You do amazing work, Jaheim. I will definitely recommend you to anyone."

"I appreciate that, lil mama. Come on. You gotta date to get ready for."

Like the true gentleman I am, I opened the car door for Aaliyah and let her get in on the driver's side of her car. Closing the door, I jogged to the passenger side and got in as Aaliyah drove back around to the front of the shop.

"What the fuck?" Aaliyah and I looked on as Brandon and Keith were holding back two women. Taking a closer look, it was Regina and Aaliyah's friend.

"Oh my god, Chantelle!" I heard Aaliyah yell as she got out of her car. I ran towards the fight to help control the girls. "God damn it, Regina! What the fuck are you doing here?"

"Fuck You Jah, you mean to tell me you had this bitch here the whole time and didn't bother to call me so that I could beat this hoe's ass."

"They just got here, and no, I wasn't gone call you because like I said yesterday you deserved to get your ass beat."

I looked over, and Aaliyah was having a hard time calming who I now knew as Chantelle down. I ran over to try to diffuse the situation.

"Aaliyah, I am sorry. I did not know she was coming here."

"I know you didn't. I need to get her out of here. I will see you tonight."

I watched as they speed out of my parking lot, I just hopped this little situation doesn't ruin our night. I could hear Regina still cussing me out. I walked off ignoring her dumb ass. My cousins were a big reason why my ex and I had such a nasty break up by being so messy and petty. They would often invite her out with them, and she was the type who couldn't control herself when she was drinking. She cheated and brought me home something. Thank God it was curable, but still, she did me foul, nonetheless, so shit ended. She tried to blame me, but I never cheated. She eventually came clean and tried to get back with me, but by that time, I was like fuck bitches. I always felt that if she wasn't so influenced by my cousins to go out, so much shit might have ended differently.

After today my mind had been made up, I had to cut my cousins off. I sacrificed and dealt with too much. I needed to have a talk with my aunt and let her know I was done with they shit. I didn't know how she would take it, but it needed to be done. I made it back to my office to pack up my things and head home. I wanted tonight to go as smoothly as possible with Aaliyah. I locked up and headed to my car. "Aye, Jah, hold up!" I turned around and saw Brandon running towards me.

"What up, Brandon?"

"Shit. Making sure you straight, I finally got your hot-headed ass cousin to calm down and leave. Damn, that girl is hell."

"Yeah all of them are just the fucking same."

"True, but when did you start dating fat bitches?"

"Man, Brandon, watch your fucking mouth! Aaliyah is not a bitch for one, and for two, that's your problem. You're always looking at the wrong thing. She must not have been that fat, you were fucking with her weren't you?"

"Man, that hoe was a quick fuck, and that's it, but shit, do you nigga. If you like the big bitches ok, but I'm out. Don't let her big ass eat the entire restaurant."

I looked on as Brandon walked off. He had to be one of the most ignorant niggas ever. The shit he was saying was straight trash.

The dumb shit wasn't about to stop my date with Aaliyah. Fuck

Brandon and his dumb ass way of thinking, fucking clown. I walked

to my car thinking of ways to impress my future lady tonight.

Aaliyah

I swear I was so fucking pissed right now. From the dumb shit that Brandon said to the way Chantelle that flip the fuck out on ole girl. Why this shit had to fucking go down, and of all things, Brandon and Jah were fucking co-workers. I wondered how close they were. I didn't need any drama in my life.

I made it back to my house with Chantelle speeding right behind me. I knew she was pissed, but I didn't give a damn. I wasn't bailing her dumb ass out of jail because of Demario's fuck boy ass.

"So you really going out with this nigga knowing his bitch ass cousin is the reason me and Demario ain't together no more?"

"See Chantelle that's where you are wrong. Demario is the reason y'all not together anymore. He's the one who cheated, so why wouldn't I go out with Jaheim? He hasn't done shit to you or Demario."

"Because Aaliyah, we are girls, best friends, if I got beef with someone, you're supposed to have my back."

"No Chantelle. I got your back no matter what, and I always keep it one hundred with you, but why do I have to sacrifice my happiness because you decided to be with cheating ass Demario. The first time he cheated should have been the last time."

"You are not getting the point, Aaliyah. This bitch was fucking with my man, and she just happened to be cousins with the man you been stalking. Once that shit was revealed, you should have said no. You see how bad Demario and that bitch hurt me, and you fucking with the bitch's family."

"Chantelle, you sound real stupid right now. Demario and that girl been fucking around. That has nothing to do with Jaheim and me, so if you don't mind, I have to get ready."

I swear Chantelle was tripping, I couldn't believe the dumb shit she was saying. Why should I have to cancel my plans because of her drama? I honestly couldn't see how she thought that was going to make everything better. I had to deal with the fact that Brandon and Jah not only knew each other but were co-workers. I didn't have no type of feelings for Brandon or no shit like that, but I knew how niggas in the hood operated. They love talking down on a female and making her look bad to the next nigga. That's the type of boy Brandon was, and for him to call me fat was a low blow.

I have always struggled with my weight. I embrace it now, and I love my curves, but I was always considered a big girl. In my younger days, I was often body shamed for being overweight. I tried everything from diets, fat burning pills, to damn near starving myself, but nothing seemed to give me the immediate results that I was looking for. So, I fell into a deep depression.

I met Brandon and thought he was really for me. He told me he was always attracted to bigger women and of course, the naïve me believed the shit he said. He played me like a fool for two years until I bossed up a left his dog ass, so I've been single and crushing on Jaheim ever since. In the meantime, I managed to tone up a little, but I still had curves, and I was satisfied with myself.

I decided that I was going to put the events from today in the back of my mind and enjoy my night with Jaheim. We were going to City Grill, which was one of my favorite restaurants. They served the best grilled chicken salad ever, and the drinks were top shelf and amazing. Choosing the right outfit was going to be my main issue, I wanted to look classy, sexy, and be warm all in one. The last few nights have been extremely cold and tonight was no different. It was damn near 30 degrees outside. Being from the south, that shit is cold, so I knew whatever I choose boots would be the footwear for the evening.

After 30 minutes of searching, I decided on a pair of distressed jeans, a black and gold wrap sweater that hung slightly off my shoulder, and a pair of four-inch black ankle length boots. I picked out a gold and black panty and bra set. I set the mood by playing my Boyz II Men playlist. Grabbing my Moonlight Path shower gel and lotion, I headed to my bathroom.

An hour later, I was fully dressed and just needed to finish up my hair and makeup. I put a few tight curls in my hair and finger combed them out. I also made sure my edges and sides were laid properly. I little eyeliner, gold eye shadow, and MAC nude lip gloss and I was ready and looking damn good. My skin was glowing, and I was feeling myself. I took one good look in my full body mirror and snapped a few selfies for my social media accounts. I was really feeling myself. By the time I was finished, it was a little after nine. I grabbed my phone and keys and went to my living room.

Looking at my phone, I saw that Jaheim sent me a text letting me know he was three minute away. Of course, my stomach decided to start doing butterflies. I said a quick prayer that everything went perfectly tonight. I grabbed my things and headed outside. As soon as I opened the door, Jaheim was walking to my doorstep. This man looked so good dressed in a pair of khaki slacks, a cream-colored Polo sweater, a pair of wheat Timbs, and a leather jacket. His dreads were pulled back in a ponytail. I could stare at this man for days at a time. That's how sexy he was.

"You ready to go?" I heard Jaheim's sexy as baritone voice say to me.

"Yes, I am." I had to struggle to find my voice so that I could answer him.

Jaheim grabbed my hand and led me to his car. Like a true gentleman, he opened my door allowing me to get in and closing the door. I watched as he walked around to the driver's side of the car and got in. The drive to the restaurant was a 30-minute drive. I wasn't pleased with his choice of music. Jaheim was from hood, and he let that shit be known. So we listened to Kevin Gates on the way to the restaurant. I was not a fan of today's rap music. I tried listening to it, but I couldn't get into it at all no matter how hard I tried. However, looking over at Jaheim, he was feeling it. I heard stories about how Jah would handle niggas that disrespected him or his family. That shit was a turn on to me.

"Is your homegirl good? I honestly didn't know my cousin was going to show up today."

"She is pissed off at me at the moment, but she will be just fine."

"Why is she mad at you, because you wouldn't let her fight?"

"She feels that with you being related to ole girl, I don't have her back and should have canceled my plans with you. I told her she sounded stupid and that you and I have nothing to do with her and that dumbass ex of hers. After that, I left her standing outside looking crazy."

"That's real fucked up, I can't control my cousin or that dumb nigga, and neither can you."

"I know that's what I told her. I understand she's hurting right now, but she is taking it out on the wrong people, and I stood behind her the last time Demario did some dumb shit. I was ready to bail her out of jail, but the girl and Demario didn't press charges, and their injuries weren't life threating, so they didn't keep her."

"Damn, she was wilding like that?"

"What she did to your cousin was nothing. Now Demario ass got fucked up again like last time. Last time the dumb nigga suffered a broken elbow and all."

I laughed as I told Jah the story of Chantelle's crazy ass. My girl is truly was a nut case. We arrived at the restaurant, and thankfully, it wasn't crowded. With it being so cold outside, I didn't anticipate a huge crowd anyway.

"So what's good on the menu?"

"I like the grilled chicken salad with extra onions and peppers."

"That sounds good. I prefer steak tho."

"I believe you can add steak, and the drinks are top shelf and so good."

"That's what's up."

"So how long have you had your shop?"

"I have had this shop for about two years. I am in the process of expanding to my second location not far from here.'"

"That's what's up. Jaheim, a businessman. I love to see black men owning and operating their own business."

"Thanks, lil mama."

"So how long has Brandon's bitch ass worked for you?"

"About a year, and why that man gotta be all that?"

Because he is, fuck him tho."

"Damn, lil mama, you really hate him?"

"I damn near do. He said some fucked up shit today when he for one knows that I have had issues with my body."

"I don't see any problem with your body, trust me."

When our food came, we sat and enjoyed our food and drinks. I was damn near in tears as I told him my struggles with my weight and depression dealing with my weight. The way he sat and listened to me showed me that he was really hearing me. I have always had a way of telling if people were really listening to me it not. Jaheim looked me in my eyes as I spoke, and he grabbed my hand as I was near tears. For years I felt like no one understood how I felt. I felt alone for so long, and after losing my mother, that was the lowest I have ever felt.

That's why I was so sure that Brandon was really into me. Brandon had a way of making me feel wanted and important. He would never tell me I was beautiful, but he was always around me. We went out a few times, but never where it was really crowded. We would go to late night movies or restaurants that weren't that popular. Of course, I never really thought much of it. He was just spending time with me as a boyfriend should. I started to get suspicious of Brandon when we would start having his phone face down or would turn to the side whenever his phone would ring. I was never the type to go through my man phone, but curiosity got the best of me, and like the old saying goes *keep searching, and you're going to find something you don't want to see,* and that's what happened.

I found phone numbers text from different females, nudes of him and different females. Brandon was really out there acting single. After that I refused to continue to be his test dummy, I honestly didn't care if I was single or not, in my opinion being single was a hell of a lot better than being played and looking like a dummy. After seeing that shit, that's when I decided to leave Brandon and focus on me for now on. Brandon came home one day, and all his shit was packed up in bags and left by the door, I turned off the cell phone I was paying for and made sure he handed over the keys to my car that he was driving around the city in with other bitches. The night I ended things with Brandon was ugly.

"Yeah Chantelle, I am waiting on his bitch ass now to bring my car back, and I got something for his ass. I can believe he was playing me, and for two years at that. How could I be that dumb?"

"Listen, Aaliyah. You weren't being dumb. Brandon is just that damn good at being a dog."

"I think that's him now, Chantelle. Let me call you back."

I sat down on the chair with a glass of wine and waited on Brandon bitch ass to walk in the house, but I had a surprise for his ass. He was going to walk right into all of his shit packed in trash bags.

"Aaliyah, why the fuck are all these bags in the doorway? I almost broke my damn leg."

"That was the point."

"The fuck you mean, that was the point?"

"What I said, the point was for you to trip and break something, you dog ass nigga. Give me my fucking car keys, call your people, and get the fuck out of my house. I will not be your fucking fool any longer. I know everything, and I have the proof, so don't try to lie your way out of nothing. Just get your shit and get the fuck out, right fucking now!"

"Aaliyah, baby, what is going on with you? Why are you acting like this?"

"I knew you would play dumb, so that's why I was prepared for you and your excuses. Who is Star? Who is Aniyah? Who is Samantha? Do these names ring a bell to you, Brandon? The must since they all through your messages, showing titties and pussy. They must sound familiar. You done fucked all of them, and Latoya was lucky enough to get a weekend vacation to the beach. My question to you Brandon is how long did you expect to keep this shit up, huh? Did you think I would never find out is that what it is? Well, guess what, I found the fuck out, and I am done with you, and I suggest you find a way to pay your phone bill cause after tonight you are off my account and your phone will be off."

"You say that shit like your fat ass mean it, who the fuck gone put up with your fat ass? I'm the only nigga you gone ever have, so you might as well put my shit back where it came from cause I ain't leaving shit!"

"See, Brandon, I knew you would do some dumb shit like this, so of course, I came prepared. My brother is two houses down, and I let him know that if you and your shit were not gone out of my house

in 30 minutes from the time you got here to come and beat your ass cause you got 15 minutes left to get the fuck out."

"Fuck you, you fat ass bitch! Good luck finding a fucking man to look at you, stupid bitch!"

That night I cried so hard, not because I was now single, or because of the break up with Brandon, in all honesty, the way Brandon was acting I was single for a long time, but because I was free and done with dealing with the bullshit. I told myself I would never let a man make me feel less than a woman. I started working out at my own pace and dieting the best way for me. I was going to do this at my own pace and do it for me.

"Damn, I didn't know Brandon was like that."

"He is the worst. I just refuse to entertain his bullshit anymore."

Jaheim and I finished our food and drinks and were headed back home. I wish the night didn't have to end, but I had to work tomorrow, and so did Jah. By the time we arrived back to my house, I was starting to feel the effects of the alcohol, I wasn't drunk, but I was a little tipsy, so I was ready for my bed.

"Did you enjoy your food, Jaheim?"

"I did. For my first time there, the shit was good, and I'm definitely going back."

"Good, I am glad you enjoyed it."

"You feeling kind of nice, huh?"

"Just a little bit, maybe I shouldn't have had that last shot Patrón, but I'm good tho."

"Umm, ok cause your eyes look a little low and sexy over there."

"Ok Jaheim, don't start nothing we not gone finish."

"Nah lil mama, trust me. If I start it, I'm most definitely going to finish it trust me, baby girl."

I looked at Jaheim as he drove back towards my house and I could see myself riding shotgun with this man often as his woman. I just prayed he enjoyed his night just as much as I did.

"You know this is the first real date I have been on since breaking up with Brandon's bitch ass."

"That just means that you were waiting for the right man to come along and show you how it's done."

"So does that mean you are the right man, Jah?"

"I don't know, lil mama, am I?"

"Yeah, you are."

I couldn't believe my drunk ass just said that. I looked over at Jaheim to see if I could read his expression on his face, and of course, it was expressionless. I could feel my depression start to kick in, so I just sat up in my seat and looked out the window as we drove. I have seen this street so many times, but right now, things were looking different to me. I was getting depressed, and I didn't know why. It was only our first date, and things went great, so I didn't know why maybe it was because I was feeling him and wanted him to like me. I needed to get myself together and fast.

Arriving back at my house, I started to feel more relaxed. I was home and in my comfort zone. I opened the car door and walked to my doorstep with Jaheim on my trails. Stopping to grab my keys, I felt Jaheim grab me by the shoulder and turn me around. I tried my hardest not to look him in his eyes because I knew if I did it I was going to break. Deep down I still suffered from depression and seeing Brandon and hearing these hurtful things he said brought back a lot of emotions and pain. I was still broken. I just hid it so well.

"Talk to me, lil mama. You got real quiet in the car and look at me when you speak."

I looked at Jaheim and tried to find the right words to say. I didn't want to run him off by telling him about my sudden bout of depression, but I wanted to be honest with him. I contemplated just telling him that I was fine, but he could tell if I was lying.

"Don't just stand there Aaliyah, talk to me. Matter of fact, let's go inside and just talk."

We walked into my house, and Jaheim took a seat. I told him to make himself comfortable while I went to the back to change myself. I decided a tee shirt and a pair of tights would have to work. I washed my makeup off and wrapped my hair. I figured if we were going to have this conversation, then I might well be relaxed as ever.

I took my time and walked back out to the living room. Jaheim was texting on his phone when I sat down beside him. With my feet tucked under me, I looked at Jaheim and began to just pour my heart out.

"I still suffer from depression. Seeing Brandon today and hearing the hurtful things he was saying brought back a lot of pain. Sometimes it doesn't really bother me, but I guess today because he was saying it in front of you made me a little embarrassed. Like I told you, I have always had problems with my weight, and sometimes I get depressed thinking about my struggles."

"I still suffer from depression myself sometimes. I lost both of my parents on the same day when I was a child. After losing my cousin to the streets, I was mad at the world. All I wanted was revenge for his death and for the pain that I was in. I was in a relationship at the time with my ex Shane' and shit was all bad. My cousins heavily influenced her. They would always go clubbing and shit like that. She was the type who couldn't control her alcohol. She would often flirt with different niggas and allow niggas to touch and feel all on her like that shit was cool. That shit wasn't cool to me. We would have arguments and fights, and she would always say she was done and it wouldn't happen again. That shit was a fucking lie. I caught the bitch bent over one of the couches in VIP in the club. Shit was fucked up. Let's just say I tore the club up. The bitch was done then it wasn't nothing else she could say to me ever. After that, it was fuck bitches. Get my money and fuck 'em.

"Damn Jaheim, I am sorry to hear that."

"You don't need to apologize lil mama. You didn't do anything. It sounds to me like the shit Brandon put you through is still fucking with your mental, and I can't tell you not to let it, but just know I think that you are beautiful and sexy as fuck. Your curves will turn any man on. Shit, my dick is getting hard just thinking about the shit.

"Thank you."

"No thanks needed, but I am about to head on out. I'm gone hit you when I get to the crib."

I walked Jah to the door and watched as he walked to the car. Closing the door behind me, I just stood there for a moment. The words he was saying to me were replaying heavily in my mind. Maybe

I was still fucked up about Brandon and my past. I just prayed that I would be able to trust again. It's easy to smile on the outside and still be hurting on the inside, and that's exactly what was happening to me. I went back into my bedroom said my prayers and laid down. I asked God to help me get over this pain and depression.

Jaheim

I really enjoyed my night with Aaliyah shit was mad cool. I haven't taken a woman on a date since Shanae' and the vibe was dope. Her opening up to me showed me that she was really feeling a nigga. After dropping Aaliyah off, I headed back to the crib. Tomorrow was going to be an extremely busy day. Tomorrow was the deadline for me to choose my new manager for my second location. I still had not made my decision on whether I would be keeping my cousin on or not. My gut was telling me just to let her go because shit wasn't gone change.

I made it home and like always, I grabbed my piece from under the seat and stepped out. Although I didn't live in the hood any longer, I still didn't trust motherfuckers. You never knew when or if a nigga was lurking, and I for sure wasn't trying to be caught slipping. I checked my surroundings and made my way in the house. I placed my keys down and headed to the back. It was already one o'clock in the morning, and a nigga was tired. I said a quick prayer up to the man above and laid my ass down. It was back to the money tomorrow, and a nigga was ready to stack up.

***

The next morning I woke up and did my normal morning routine. I made sure to send Aaliyah a good morning message and told her to have a good day. I wanted her to know that she was on my mind when I woke up this morning. Shit, I hadn't even gotten the pussy yet, and I was doing all this love shit, but lil mama was different, and I was attracted to her. For me, it wasn't just her body but also her spirit. She was beautiful inside and out, and I wanted to make sure she knew that. From our talk last night, I could tell that she was still hurt from the shit she went through with that nigga Brandon. She opened up to me a lot, and I could hear her pain. I finished getting ready and headed out the door.

I wanted to get to the shop early. My mind was made up, and I was letting Cherie go. I was going to offer the manager/front desk position for this store to Erica and the same position of my second location to Stacey. They were the two best qualified candidates for the position. I knew this choice would hurt my aunt, but I had to do what was best for me and my business. I called up both candidates and made an appointment for them to both meet me today at three o'clock. That gave me enough time to have everything prepared and ready for them to sign.

I had been in my office for a little over an hour when I saw Cherie come in, just like every morning, the first thing she did was turn on her music and plug up her phone, put her bag away, and head to the break room. I waited to see how long it would take her to start up her computers and actually begin work. Thirty minutes passed, and she was still in the breakroom. The store was set to open in fifteen minutes, and she wasn't prepared for anything. Today was going to be her last day, no questions asked.

"Jah, good morning, what's good boss man?" I looked up and saw Brandon standing in my office door texting on his phone.

"Aye, Brandon, good morning. How you doing, man?"

"Shit good with me, how did your date with my ex ole fat ass?"

"Man, stop calling my girl fat, stop all that shit."

"Oh, she's your girl now? You just gone fuck with her knowing I was fucking with her?"

"And why wouldn't I, Brandon? Like you said she is your ex meaning y'all ain't together no more. Aaliyah is free game, my nigga."

"Man, fuck all that. That's my girl, so you shouldn't be even entertaining her!"

"Nah, she was your girl, and you fucked that shit up. You broke her, but it's gone take a real nigga like me to fix her. All you did was try to make her not trust any other nigga, but I came along and changed that. So, she is not your girl, but she is gone be mine once I pick up the broken pieces that you left."

"Man, Jah, fuck all that poetic, love shit. You gone see. She's coming back to me, just watch/"

"You funny man, she won't go back to a boy, trust me. Now if you would excuse me, I have work to do and so do you."

I watched as Brandon walked off talking shit under his breath. The lil nigga couldn't fuck with me. He knew my track record and how the fuck I got down. The shit he was saying was just dumb as fuck. It was dudes like him that woman didn't trust niggas now. Men like him broke good females just to make themselves look good. I wasn't about to allow that nigga to fuck up my day. Pushing that shit to the back of my mind, I continued my day.

***

My day continued to go as smoothly as I imagined. We were packed with cars and business was going good. I had the meeting with the two positions, and thankfully, they both said yes. Now I just needed to break the news to my cousin. I had been so busy today I didn't get a chance to check my phone to see if Aaliyah had messaged me back from this morning. I grabbed my phone and opened my Facebook app. I smiled looking at the message from lil mama.

Aaliyah James: Good morning, Jaheim. I hope that you have a great day at work as well. Thank you for last night. I really had a great time and thanks for listening to me.

Jaheim Martin: No thanks, lil mama, I appreciate you opening up to me. Can I see you tonight?

Aaliyah James: Sure where would you like to meet?

Jaheim Martin: I was thinking you could come by my spot, and I could cook you dinner

Aaliyah James: I would like that.

Jaheim Martin: Aight then, I will see you tonight at eight. I will text you the address.

I locked my phone and continued my day. I watched as Cherie didn't do anything all day. She was giving customers attitude, slacking on service, and her workstation was a complete mess. It was time to let her go and start fresh Monday morning.

"Cherie, could you please come into my office."

"I was just headed out for the night. What's up, Jah?"

"Cherie I'm not beating around the bush, I am letting you go. Today was your last day. You barely do any work, you give attitude to the customers, your area is always a mess, and I am tired of you and your ratchet ass sisters using my place of business as your own personal gossip lounge. Now, I will provide you with your last paycheck, but as of now you are fired."

"How the fuck you gone fire me Jah, your own flesh and blood, who the fuck in supposed to replace me and how you gone explain this to my mama?"

"I already have your replacement, and I will handle Aunt Sarah. This has nothing to do with family. This is strictly business."

"Fuck you, Jaheim! Go to hell just watch how this place goes down when I leave!"

The last thing I wanted to do was fire my cousin, but I had to do what was best for my company and me. Everyone had gone home for the weekend, so I closed up my shop and headed home. I was meeting lil mama in a few hours, and I really wanted to impress her.

Chantelle

"**A**aliyah, I am not mad at you at all. I am just hurt with everything going on I honestly feel that you were taking sides by choosing him over me."

"Chantelle, I wasn't choosing Jah over you, but some of the shit you said was fucked up, and you know it."

"Look, I am sorry Aaliyah. Can we just go out tonight and talk?"

"I can't tonight. Jaheim invited me over to his place for dinner, and I already said yes to him, but we can do something tomorrow. I am off, and we can spend the entire day together."

"No, that's fine. I'm good, Aaliyah. Enjoy your night."

I hung up the phone with Aaliyah feeling even more depressed than before. I was really fucked up over Demario. I did everything to mold his dumb ass into the best man possible and for him to just fuck any bitch. Hell, if he was going to cheat, at least cheat with a bitch that looks halfway decent, damn girl looks like a chia pet, and he had the nerve to have her sucking his dick at a party. I should have killed them both when I had the chance. I was so in love with Demario. Even after he cheated the first time, I let him come back into my life. That was a fucking mistake. Right now, I felt so alone I needed my best friend, but she didn't have time for me. I know I was being selfish, but I needed her.

I looked at my phone and realized that I had been sitting in this parking lot for over an hour. I haven't been home in three days, so it was time for me to head home and try and fix the broken pieces of my life. I rode in silence with just my thoughts in my head. I kept replaying some of the messages I saw in Demario's phone and got pissed off all over again. I swear I wanted to kill his ass. That gash in his forehead wasn't enough.

I was so fucking mad that I hadn't realized I drove straight to that his house. I saw his car in the yard, so I knew his dumb ass was home. I got out the car and grabbed my keys to let myself in. I figured his dumb ass was either in there smoking or sleep. Walking in, I didn't see him in his usual spot on the couch smoking a blunt, so I walked a little further in the house. I stopped at the bedroom because that's where I heard. I put my ear to the door, and my heart broke even more. I couldn't believe he was in there fucking another girl. My first thought was just to walk away and end things for good, but I needed to know why. Why would he do me like this after everything I did for him, how could he do this to me?

"Ohhh Mario, right there daddy. Don't stop! Ohhhh, Mario, I love you! Oh god, I love you, baby!"

"I love you too, Star! I'm bout to nut. Damn girl, I'm bout to nut….ahhhhhh shit, girl! Damn, you got some good pussy!"

"Oh my god Mario, that shit was good. I love you, baby."

"Damn, I love you too, Star!"

"You love her? You fucking love her, Mario? How the fuck you love her when just last week we were talking marriage?"

"Fuck Chantelle, how did you get in here, and what the fuck are you doing here?"

"I got a key remember you, dumb fuck. Oh, you thought I was at work huh, well surprise motherfucker, I'm fucking here!"

"Demario, who the fuck is this and why does she have a key to your house and I don't?"

"Star, shut the fuck up, please. Just shut the fuck up, let me talk to her."

"Chantelle, baby, come on let's talk, please. We can work this out. I am sorry!"

"Man fuck you and your fucking sorrys nigga! You're not even worth my time anymore and most definitely not my freedom. Fuck you Mario, and I hope your dick falls off. Oh, and Star, is that your name? You're not the only one. Ask him about Regina, that the bitch who was sucking his dick a few nights ago. Unlike her, I'm not gone fuck your shit up or fuck you up. If you want his cheating ass, you can fucking have him!"

And like that I was out the door, I held my tears until I got in my car, and then I just let them out, It would be a while before I would be the same again. I spent so much time with Demario that I now needed to focus on me. This would be my first Valentine's Day alone. I just prayed I was strong enough to stay away from Demario and not run back to him.

I made it back to my house and climbed right into bed. I turned my phone off and tuned the world out. All I could do was cry and release all of this pain. I cried until I cried myself to sleep, and I think I even cried in my sleep. I needed it to get through this and be strong for myself. Fuck love, I was done with that shit forever.

Aaliyah

I was in the middle of getting ready for my second date with Jaheim. Tonight he invited me over to his place, and he was going to cook for me. I was so excited to spend more time with Jah. We really hit it off last night, and I wanted to continue that. I honestly didn't mean to get so deep into my life with him last night, but Jah has a way of making you speak up and say what's on your mind. I wasn't used to that. Brandon never really listened to me, and I noticed that with Jaheim he really listens. He looks you directly in your eyes as you speak. My nerves were getting the best of me, but I was trying my hardest not to let that happen.

I wanted to be comfortable tonight, so I dressed in something simple. I wore a pair of black tights and black Champion sweater, and some black A1's on my feet. I sprayed my favorite Bath and Body Works spray all over, and I was headed out the door. I didn't know what to expect tonight with Jaheim, but whatever was going to happen I was all for it. I drove the 20-minute ride to Jaheim's house with my R&B playlist on my iPhone. Right now "Gotta Be" by Jagged Edge was playing as I drove, and thoughts of Jaheim were in my head. I'd had a crush on him for so long. Seeing him in the hood was the highlight of my day. We would often make eye contact, but I never thought anything of it. I would just dream about him and fantasize about things he would do to me. I wanted this man in the worst way for so long, and now here I was on my way to his house for dinner.

I arrived at Jaheim's house, and of course, my stomach decided to do backflips. I needed to calm down and just breathe. I sent Jaheim a text message to let him know I was outside. I placed my phone in my jacket pocket and walked up the driveway. For a single man, Jaheim had a beautiful house. The yard was clean with not a leave sight. He even had little lawn decorations in the yard. Little tea lights finished off the walkway. By the time, I made it to the door, Jah was already on the porch waiting on me. He looked so fine in a black wife beater and some gray sweats. My eyes couldn't miss the nice size bulge that was showing through his sweats. "Come on in and make yourself comfortable. Dinner is almost ready."

"Oh, thank you. It smells good, what are you cooking?"

"I am making my famous shrimp and chicken Alfredo with garlic toast and roasted parmesan asparagus."

"Oh wow, that sounds amazing! I can't wait to eat."

"Can I offer you something to drink? I have wine, water, juice, and soda, I have liquor but its Hennessey, and I remember you saying Patrón was your favorite."

"Yes, I don't like Hennessey, so wine would be fine."

"Coming right up."

Looking around Jaheim's house, you could tell that a man lived there. There was not a hint of a female touch anywhere in sight. Jaheim had a huge 60-inch TV mounted on the wall, and he had *SportsCenter* playing on it. He had a nice bar area with what looked like shot glasses from every professional football and basketball team. I didn't know much about basketball, but I knew for sure that he all thirty-two football teams on his bar. I wondered if he was a collector. His living room was not over furnished. He had a leather sectional and a coffee table. You could see his kitchen from his living room, and he had all state of the art kitchen appliances. The way he moved around in the kitchen, you would think that Jaheim was a Bobby Flay or some shit. He was stirring pots and flipping shrimp as if he was on *Iron Chef*.

"Here you go Aaliyah. Dinner is served."

"Thank you so much, and it looks delicious."

"I hope you enjoy, lil mama."

"So tell me how your day was, Aaliyah?"

"My day was ok. I worked, and of course, this time of year my store was crazy packed, we have our annual Valentine's sale going on along with the semi-annual sale, so we are packed from open to close."

"That's right you work at Bath and Body Works, right. I have been in there to buy my aunt a few things. She likes their candles and shit. My ex Shanae' used to wear this stuff call Sweet Pea or some shit."

I laughed at Jaheim trying to name the different fragrance we sold. Sweet Pea was one of our oldest scents, and we still sold it to this day.

"I'm not really a fan of Sweet Pea. My favorite is Moonlight Path."

"Ok, I have never heard if that."

"I am actually wearing it now."

"Seriously that shit smells good."

"Thanks, Jaheim."

"No thanks needed lil mama. I only speak facts."

Jaheim and I finished our dinner and made our way back to the living room. Jaheim really surprised me with his music section for the night. Tonight he had Usher's *8701* album playing which was one of my favorite Usher albums ever. "How Do You Say" was my shit.

"I didn't know you liked Usher."

"What you mean, my music choice is very diverse. I listen to anything that sounds good. I bet you thought because I'm a hood nigga all I listened to was trap music, nah lil mama I like it all, except country and heavy metal. I can't fuck with that shit."

"I like country believe it or not, but not so much rap or trap whatever it's called, I can't get into it at all."

"You gotta give it a try lil mama, not all of it is bad. Some actually sound good."

"Maybe one day I will, I don't know, Jah."

"Aaliyah let me ask you a personal question."

"Umm ok, what is it?"

"When was the last time you been with a man?"

"Not since Brandon, why are you asking?"

"Lil mama, I don't beat around the bush. I want you bad. My dick has been bricking up since you walked in here in those tights on. I don't want to just fuck you. I want to take my time and explore your entire body— every curve, every dimple, every mark. I want to get to know every part of your body. If you don't want to take there it's cool, my feelings won't change, and we can continue to get to know each other until you're ready."

"I want you too, Jaheim. I have dreamed about being with you, and I am ready."

Jaheim took my hand and led me to his bedroom. His king size bed was neatly made in all black bed set. His entire bedroom was black. The carpet on the floor, the curtains, and even his dressers were black. By this time, the music had changed from Usher to Joe.

As Joe's "Love Scene" played through the speakers, Jaheim kissed me. His lips were so soft, and I could taste the Hennessey and the Winterfresh gum on his breath. I wrapped my arms around his neck and kissed him back, welcoming his tongue in my mouth. As we continued our kiss, Jaheim laid me on the bed and began kissing my body. He started from my neck down to my chest and my stomach. While one hand caressed my breasts, he used the other to pull down my tights.

"Take everything off, Aaliyah. I want to see your entire body."

"I'm ashamed of my body, Jaheim."

"You don't have to be ashamed in front of me. I am not Brandon. I want to see you, so like I said, strip."

I began to take off my clothes as Jaheim looked on at me. I started with my tights and then my shirt. I was standing there in my bra and panties with my hands covering my body.

"Move your hands Aaliyah and take everything off."

I stepped out of my panties and removed my bra. I couldn't believe I was standing here with Jaheim in nothing but my birthday suit.

"You are so fucking beautiful, Aaliyah, you have nothing to be ashamed of your body is a temple and right now, I want to explore that temple."

Jaheim laid me on the bed and began kissing me again. This time he kissed down to my pussy. Jaheim spread both of my legs and kissed the inside of both of my thighs. As Jaheim kissed my thighs, I felt him place two fingers inside of me and used his tongue to send me spinning.

"Ahhhh Jahhhh, that feels so good!"

"Damn, this pussy taste good! Damn, lil mama!"

I grabbed Jaheim by his dreads as he continued his oral assault on my pussy. I came three times before he stopped. I watched as Jaheim reached in his dresser and grabbed a Magnum. Pulling off his sweats, my eyes had to be playing tricks on me. Jaheim's dick I know was at least 11inches or more. My mouth began watering just looking at it. Brandon was big, but he had nothing on Jaheim.

"Don't look so shocked, lil mama. Big boys don't carry little dicks. This is all me, baby."

I bit my lower lip as I watched Jah place the condom on his dick, he rolled the condom on and made sure it was on and secured. Climbing back on the bed he used his knee to spread my legs apart, and he kissed me slowly as he entered inside me. I arched my back to allow him to put his entire dick inside of me."

"OH MY GOD, JAHHHHHH!!!"

"Talk to me, lil mama, how does it feel?"

"Jah, you feel so good! You feel so fucking good, Jaheim!"

"Damn lil mama. Your pussy is so tight and wet. God damn lil mama, I could never get enough of this pussy!"

"I'm about to cum, Jah! I'm cumming!"

"Cum for me, lil mama, let big daddy feel it!"

"Jahhhhhhh, I'm cumming!!! Don't stop! Please, don't stop!!"

"Come ride this dick, lil mama."

I did as Jah told me to do, and I swear this felt better than missionary position. I threw my head back as I rode Jaheim's dick. The way he grabbed me by my waist and sucked my breasts let me know that he was enjoying the ride. A few minutes later, we were switching positions again. This time Jah instructed me to get on my knees and arch my back. I spread my legs and gave my back the perfect arch, allowing Jaheim to put everything he had inside of me. As soon as he put his dick in, I was cumming. I came so hard that I was praying that Jah was on the verge of cumming. His stamina was on point, and his sex game was A1."

"Damn lil mama I'm bout to nut, cum with me. God damn baby, your shit is the truth."

Jaheim and I laid there just staring at each other both of us lost in our own thoughts and emotions. I just prayed that I hadn't made a mistake by sleeping him so quickly. I don't think I could handle any more rejection and I really liked Jaheim.

"So what now, Jaheim?"

"What you mean what now? We are trying to see where this relationship is going to go. You thought that I was just gone fuck you and tell you to leave. That's not me, lil mama. If I just wanted to fuck, I would have fucked you on the floor in the living room. I wanted to explore your body for a reason. I wanted to know which spots to kiss turn you on, and which position had you cumming the most. By exploring your body, I know where to touch and not touch. If I just wanted to fuck, I would have taken you to a hotel and fucked you, but I didn't. I want you, lil mama. I'm not saying this relationship is going to be easy. We have both been through heartache and pain, so of course, both of our guards will be up, and our trust will be strained, but if you give me a chance to help you heal your heart, you can help heal mine as well."

"I'm willing to see where this goes, Jaheim. I have suffered from depression for so long, and I have a fear of commitment. Just work with me, please. That's all that ask."

"I will give you more than that, Aaliyah."

That night I decided to give love another shot. I didn't know where this was going to go, but I wanted it, and I wanted it with Jaheim.

Jaheim

I t had been about a week since Aaliyah, and I decided to try and make this thing official. Lil mama was growing on me, and I found myself waking up with her on my mind. Every morning I woke up, I made sure to send her a good morning text to let her know that she was the first thing on my mind. Business at the shop had been crazy. The new store manager for my main store Erica was the shit with the business ideas. She came up with this customer appreciation day where loyal customers would get up to twenty percent off. We also had Working Women Wednesday where women could come in and show their proof of employment and get up to forty percent off of their car detail, which included car wash inside and outside. We would implement these ideas at our second location that was set to open in less than a month.

I finally had that talk with my aunt and let her know why I let Cherie go, and she understood completely, so that was a big burden off my back. I felt that my life was starting to get back on track. I was headed to my second location. Like I said we were set to open in less than a month and there was still so much to do before the grand opening. We were planning a huge grand opening, and I was getting excited because I would have the prettiest girl in the world on my arm. I hadn't talked to lil mama that much today. I knew she would have a busy day with work and also school was back in session, so today was her first day of class. I sent her a text just telling her I was thinking about her and to hit me up when she had a chance.

I arrived at my store and my store manager Stacey was already there and working. That's the shit that loved, a hardworking employee that didn't mind going above and beyond.

"Stacey, what's up girl? I see you in here working hard, and I appreciate that. What we got going today?"

"What's up Jaheim? You need to sign some contracts for the plumbers and electricians to come and finish the bathrooms and the outside car washing area."

"Alright cool, are they on my desk?"

"Yes, I also emailed you the rough draft for the Working Women flyer and the grand opening flyers."

"That's what's up Stacey. I appreciate that."

"And Jaheim, before you go in the back, someone is waiting for you, someone named Shanae'."

"Shanae'? What the fuck is she doing here, and how the fuck did she find me?"

"I don't know, Jah. She came here and asked for you, and I told her you weren't here, and she said you wouldn't mind if she waited."

"Ok thanks, Stacey."

What the fuck did she Shanae' want and why the fuck was she here at my shop? I needed to get her fucking gone and asap.

I walked down to my office and opened the door. My mouth dropped as I saw Shanae' sitting in my office chair in nothing but her bra and underwear. Shanae' had a body that would make a gay man straight. Her beautiful brown skin shined bright against the pink and purple bra and underwear she was wearing. With her hair pulled up in a messy bun, it highlighted her high cheekbones and dimples.

"Shanae', why are you here?"

"I came to see you Jah. I missed you."

"No the fuck you don't, so again, why the fuck are you here?"

"I'm serious Jah, I miss you baby, and I am ready to come home."

"Are you fucking serious? You're ready to come home? Bitch, your home is not with me, so I don't know what you expect but ain't shit over here for you, plus I gotta women. I'm taken."

"Yeah I saw you out with your little or should I say big girlfriend at City Grill the other night, and that's I why I figured I would come rescue you. She not right for you, baby, I am. We have always been perfect together, Jah."

"Shanae', listen to me and listen to me good. We will never be together again. I don't want you, and I don't love you. Hell, I don't even like you, so this fantasy is dead. I suggest you put your clothes on and get out before I embarrass your ass."

All I could do was laugh at Shanae's delusional ass. She honestly thought being naked in my office would make me want her back. She had to be smoking crack or some shit. I walked out of my office and back to the front. I told Stacey that if she wasn't out in ten minutes to call the cops and have them escort her ass out. I also let

Stacey know that Shanae' was banned from the property. If she steps

foot back on my property, she would be arrested.

I got back in my car, checked my phone, and saw that my lil

mama had texted me back. I also saw that I had a text from someone

that I haven't talked to in almost two years. *What the fuck does he*

want?

Snoop: Jah, what's good my nigga? I bet you're wondering

what the fuck I want huh, but check it. I got some news for you. I

got some information on the niggas that popped Kelton, and I know

the whereabouts of that bitch. Hit my line if you still trying to see

these niggas.

It had been a little over two years since Kelton got killed, and

after reading that message from Snoop, I got pissed off all over again.

I'd been looking for these niggas for almost two years. I needed to get

them niggas for Kelton. I hit Snoop back because I was game and my

trigger finger had started itching.

Me: Snoop, let's meet up to discuss business.

Snoop: Bet, give me the location, and I'm there.

Me: Meet me on the block in an hour.

Snoop: Aight, my nigga, I'll be there.

I have waited for over two years to find the motherfuckers that popped my cousin and now was the time. I was going to make they asses pay. I was so deep in thought that I didn't realize my phone was ringing. I looked down and saw that my lil mama was calling me and that instantly put a smile on my face. She had a way of making me smile just by her being in my presence or hearing her voice.

"What's up, lil mama?"

"Hey Jah, how are you?

"I'm good baby girl just leaving my second shop, where you at?"

"Leaving school, am I going to get to see you tonight?"

"Yeah, we can make something happen. Come on over to the crib. I'll hit your line when I'm home."

"Ok baby, see you later."

After hanging up with Aaliyah, I headed to the block to meet up with Snoop. I haven't been on the block in over two years, but niggas still knew who I was, and they still showed me love and respect when I came through. I wasn't no legend or shit like that, but there were stories out there about me, and that shit was true. I once shot a dude who was face down in some pussy. I told the nigga I wanted my money, and he kept giving me excuses. He always had this thing for strippers. So, I paid on of the local strippers to fuck with him. All I needed her was to give him some head and to catch that man slipping. Well, the stripper did more than that. The bitch let his ass give her some head, and when I busted in that's how I caught his ass. One shot to the dome was all it took. Either you paid me my money, or you paid with your life. I was the reason a lot of mothers and wives had to go black dress shopping. I was a ruthless motherfucker. I have since calmed down, but I would never forget where I came from.

I was the first one at the meeting spot and looking around nothing changed. Lil niggas were still on the block trying to earn their respect. Young females with barely any clothes on were still walking the block trying to catch the eyes of all the niggas on the block. The bench where I got my first blow job was still standing along with the park where I caught my first body. I hadn't moved that far from the hood, but I moved far enough to see a big difference and another side to life other than hustling. Yeah, when I was hustling, I was making pretty decent money, but now owning my own business, I make more money.

"Jaheim, the businessman, look at you nigga all GQ down and shit."

"Snoop, what's good, my nigga? You done put on some weight, boy."

"Shit, all three of my baby mamas be feeding my good, and I ain't just talking about food if you know what I mean."

"Boy, you still fucking all three baby mamas. How the hell you pull that off?

"Shit they ain't gotta know shit. I fuck one, see my kids, leave, and head to the next one house. As long as they pockets getting laced, they better not say shit to me."

"You a fool man, so what's the deal with these boys?"

"Yeah, so it's was them niggas from the west side that popped Kel man. You know my cousin Star right? Well, she's been fucking around with that nigga named Demario."

"Demario? That nigga's been fucking around with my cousin Regina and had a woman. Damn, that boy is stupid."

"Anyway Star was telling me after they finish fucking one night, they were smoking and shit and nigga told Star that he and his cousins were looking to set another nigga up just like they did Kelton two years ago."

"The fuck Snoop, I was just a party and card game with them west side niggas just last weekend, that dumb nigga got caught by his girl letting my cousin Regina suck his dick. His girl went ham on ass straight knocked his ass clean the fuck out with a glass vase."

"Oh word, my cousin Star is good for fucking with lame ass niggas."

"So, where the fuck is he at? If we can get his ass to talk, then he can let us know who did the shooting. We pop his ass for being a snitch and then go after his people."

"Jah, you think your cousin Regina could tell you where to find Demario."

"Nah, we don't need Regina. I know how to find his ass."

"How is that, Jah?"

"Remember I told you I was just at a card game and party with them west side boys last week. Well, Demario's girl who he got caught cheating on, her best friend is my girl, so I am pretty sure I can find an address. "

"Aight Jah, when you get that address, let me know so that we can get these boys."

"Aight Snoop, I'll be getting up with you soon enough."

I couldn't fucking believe it was those fucking niggas off west side and Demario's dumb ass. I knew it was a reason that I didn't like that boy.

It was getting late I needed to get back to my crib my lil mama was coming over, and I missed my girl. I was ready to dive in some pussy, and I had the perfect lady. This is what I have been waiting for, a lady to come home with every night. My life was changing, and I loved it.

Aaliyah

I was really looking forward to seeing Jaheim tonight. Today was an extremely exhausting day, and I was so glad it was over. I was glad class was back in session because that meant I only had two more semesters to go before I was finished and would have my bachelor's degree in health and human services. I would also be starting my internship at the Department of Social services next week, and I was so excited about that. Not only was my career about to take off, but I had my man too. We have only been official for a few days, but it was going so good. Jaheim was so gentle with me. He knew I had issues with depression and he would make me feel wanted and always remind me that I wasn't alone.

It was a few days before Valentine's Day, and I wouldn't be spending it alone this year, and I couldn't help but be excited. I was at home packing a bag for tonight. I planned on staying at Jaheim's house tonight. Jaheim sent me a message letting me know that he was on his way home and would pick up some food. I told him not to do that because I planned to cook for him. I knew he really loved steak, so I had gotten him two T-bone steaks, and I was going to make him some roasted potatoes to go with it. I didn't eat steak, so I was just going to order me a grilled chicken Salad from City Grill. I grabbed my Michael Kors travel bag and made sure that I had everything I needed including my Moonlight Path products and headed out the door for the night. I realized that I hadn't spoken to Chantelle in a few days, so I made a mental note to send her a text when I got to Jaheim's house. I grabbed my things and walked out the door.

"Damn, Aaliyah. That's how we do now? You just gone start dating my homeboy like we ain't been together."

I was shocked to see Brandon on my doorstep, and he had the nerve to sound upset. I honestly had to laugh to keep from getting pissed off right now. What the fuck gave him the nerve to question me, the hell was his problem?

"First of all Brandon, why the fuck are you at my house, and secondly why are you questioning me about who I am seeing? Nigga, we not together no more, and Jaheim is your boss, not your homeboy. Get that shit right."

"It doesn't matter. That's some straight hoe shit, and you know it."

"Fuck you, Brandon. That shit you did to me was straight hoe shit. So again, what do you want? I am on my way to my man, and you are pissing me off right now."

"Look, Aaliyah. I am sorry. Honestly, when I saw you at the shop looking so good, I missed you. I got mad as fuck when Jah said he was taking you out. I just want you to give me another chance. I know I fucked up bad and said some fucked up shit, but I have learned my lesson. None of them other females had anything on you, and I know that now. I am asking you to forgive me Aaliyah, and let's work things out. You don't really want Jaheim because I know you miss me, and I damn sure miss you, bae."

"Brandon, why are you doing this after two years. You now all of a sudden miss me and want me back. After two years, you need me, and you're sorry. Where the fuck was you two years ago when I was lonely and depressed thinking that I was too fat for anybody to want me? Where were you when I needed to feel wanted, and when I wanted you? Don't try that shit with me, Brandon. You don't want me, and you don't want me to be happy, and that's not fair. I would be a fool to give up what I am building with Jaheim to go back to you only for you to do me the same way. So the answer is no, I will not give you another chance, but I will say this. I forgive you, now if you would excuse me."

I walked off without allowing Brandon to say anything. The old me would have been putty in Brandon's hands and would have fallen for every word he said, but not anymore. I had a real man waiting for me, and I needed to get to him.

By the time I made it to Jaheim's house he was just pulling up himself, which was good because he could help me get these bags out of my car.

"Hey baby, you feel like helping me get these bags?"

"Sure I can do that."

"Jah, are you ok? You seem distant."

"Yeah, lil mama, I'm good. I've just a lot on my mind."

"Ok, you want to talk about it, Jah?"

"Not right now, but later. Right now I want to hear about your day."

"Alright let's go inside because I got a story to tell you."

I grabbed my overnight bag as Jah grabbed the groceries. I wasn't about to keep that little conversation with Brandon away from Jaheim because Brandon was the type of nigga that would flip shit around and make himself seem innocent.

"So babe, guess who had the nerve to show up at my house as I was leaving."

"Who?"

"Brandon. This nigga had the nerve to come to my house talking about he misses me, and he can't believe that I was going around with his homeboy and that I was in some hoe shit. So when I checked his ass, he was all sorry, and he wants me back bs. I told him he was a liar and didn't want me to be happy and that I forgave him, but he can kiss my ass on us ever being together. I told him I would be a complete dummy if I would leave you and go back to his dog ass."

"That nigga is a straight clown, lil mama. First of all, we are not homeboys. I am his boss, so he needs to stop that shit."

"I know, and that's exactly what I told him."

"Man fuck, Brandon. That nigga's a fool, but I'm gone step to him at the job when I see and let him know what we got is official and to back the fuck away. Anyway, what's up with these steaks, lil mama? Your nigga is mad hungry, and I'm trying to see what type of skills you got in the kitchen."

"I got mad skills around the kitchen, baby. You gone fall in love after I feed you."

"You done fed me the pussy, and trust me. I am in love with that shit. You got that grade A pussy that a nigga could live in forever."

"Oh my goodness, Jaheim!"

"Don't be shy, lil mama. I am only speaking facts. If the pussy good, I'm gone tell you every chance I get but listen. I am going to go answer a few emails for work, let me know when the food is done."

"Alright."

I kissed Jaheim and headed to the kitchen to cook dinner for him, I grabbed my phone and remembered to send Chantelle a text. I haven't heard from her, and I wanted to check on her. I know she was still probably upset with me, but we needed to talk and get back on track. We have had our ups and downs, and like true best friends, we always worked shit out. I connected my phone to the Bluetooth speaker that Jaheim had in his kitchen, and I let the sounds of Boyz II Men and 112 play as I prepared dinner for my man. An hour and a half later, we were seated at his dining room table enjoying a nice candlelit dinner.

"Damn Aaliyah, this steak is cooked perfectly and these potatoes, damn girl. They say a way to a man's heart is through his stomach. You must be trying to get married."

"I am glad you enjoyed it, Jah."

"Nah, lil mama, you got skills."

"Thanks, baby, so what's up? You told me you had something to tell me earlier."

"Yeah, well two years ago my cousin Kelton got murdered. He was shot while with a bitch. We always thought that he was set up because the female he was with wasn't even touched. Believe it or not,

I was a big-time hustler I done caught plenty of bodies in my day, but long story short. I found out today who the people were that killed Kelton and confirmed he was set up.

"Oh damn Jah, I am so sorry to hear that. I have heard stories about you from people, but of course, I don't know nothing about that street shit, so who are the people if you don't mind me asking?"

"Nah, here is the funny part. I know the niggas. It's them niggas from the west side. Demario's people and I were just over there the other day, that's the fucked up thing."

"Demario? What the fuck! His scary ass? That scary nigga how the hell he shot somebody? That nigga can't even fight. I done seen Chantelle beat his ass twice."

"Yeah it wasn't him but his people, and how we found out because Demario's dumb ass talk to fucking much. Apparently one of the bitches he fucking with is cousins with my homie from the block, and the bitch told him everything Demario said about the night Kelton got popped."

"I knew I didn't like that dumb motherfucker for a reason. So what you gone do, Jah?"

"Well, once I find that nigga's location and get his dumb as to talk, it's over for all of them niggas. I ain't in the streets like that no more, but I still know how shit worked. For two years I've been looking for the people that killed Kelton, and now that I know who they are, they got to fucking pay."

"But do you really want to risk it all? I mean I know that was your cousin, but look how far you have come, Jah."

"I see what you're saying Aaliyah, but they took his life for no reason. He didn't even have that much money on him, so what was the reason. They thought he had bands on him and he didn't, and when they realized that, they just shot him in cold blood."

"Damn Jah, I'm sorry. Whatever you decide to do, I will be right here, just be careful. I just got you, and I am not ready to lose you, Jaheim."

"Come here, lil mama. Listen to me. I'm not going anywhere. I promise you. You have nothing to worry about. This street never left me, and I need to get revenge for my cousin. I promised him that. So don't worry baby. I will be here with you. Now come on let's go take a shower, and let me take care of you."

"Ok, Jah."

Jaheim and I headed towards his bedroom and his master bathroom. Jaheim and I made love in the shower for the first time, and it was amazing. I was really feeling this man.

***

As Jaheim laid in the bed asleep, I said a quick prayer and asked God to watch over him. I know he was still hurting over his cousin and wanted to avenge his cousin's death, and nothing was going to stop him from doing that. I just prayed that God watched over him. I just got him in my life, and I didn't want to lose him. I looked at my phone and noticed that Chantelle had texted me back. I prayed she wasn't still mad at me. I missed my best friend, and I needed her in my life.

Bestie: Aaliyah, I am not ok. I walked in on Demario fucking some bitch named Star. I went to his house because I

wanted to talk to him and just get answers to why he chose to hurt me, and he was with her. I caught them Aaliyah, and I hate him, I want him dead. I swear I do.

Me: Chantelle, I am so sorry. I am on my way to you right now.

I locked my phone, got out the bed, and put my clothes on. I didn't want to leave Jaheim but my best friend needed me, and I needed to get to her.

"Where are you going?"

"I need to go to Chantelle. She needs me, baby. I am so sorry. She is hurting. She went by Demario's to talk to him, and she caught him and that bitch Star was fucking."

"Damn, you want me to drive you over there? I don't mind."

"No baby I'm good, but when you find that nigga Demario and get his ass to talk, make sure you shut his ass up for good as well."

I finished getting dressed, kissed Jaheim, and left. I needed to get to my best friend. She needed me, and I wasn't about to let her down.

Chantelle

I was so glad that Aaliyah was coming over. I really needed her right now. I was done with Demario. I was tired of being hurt. I wanted that nigga dead, and I was prepared to do that shit myself. Fuck Demario. He didn't deserve to live. He was poison. Love can make you do some crazy shit, but I wasn't crazy. I was dead fucking serious. I wanted that nigga dead. I needed Aaliyah to help me pull it off. I just prayed she was willing to help me.

Aaliyah got there about 30 minutes later, and I was so happy to see her, and the first thing I did was apologize to her. I said some hurtful things to her. They were said out of anger and pain. I thought she didn't have my back, but she really did. She nor Jaheim had anything to do with Demario's dumb ass.

"Hey, best friend! I missed you, Aaliyah."

"I missed you too Chantelle, and I am sorry for making you think I didn't have your back. I honestly didn't know that she was related to Jaheim."

"I know that, Aaliyah. I was just mad at the world, and I am glad you didn't let me fight that bitch cause it would have a murder scene for sure."

"Chantelle, you will get over this, I promise you that. Just give your heart time to heal and let love find you."

"I won't be happy until his bitch ass is dead, and I mean that shit. He doesn't deserve to be walking around with his poisonous dick and affecting other women."

"Chantelle, what are you talking about affecting other women."

"He gave me HIV, Aaliyah. After I went through his phone and found out about all the women he was fucking with, something told me to go get tested. It was so many women that I had to get tested. I got my results back yesterday, and I have been in this house ever since thinking of ways to kill this motherfucker. Please, Aaliyah, don't cry. I am done crying. Now I want payback, and I want it with his life because he ruined mine."

"Chantelle, I am so sorry. I don't know what to say, but I am sorry. My heart is broken. If you really want this motherfucker dead, then I am with you, and I have a plan, but you got to trust me."

Aaliyah told me everything about Demario and his cousin, and I was speechless. I had no idea that he was living foul like that, and what pissed me off even more is that he was pillow talking with this bitches. If everything worked like we planned, his bitch ass would be dead soon and very soon.

Aaliyah

I was livid right now. My best friend in the entire world now had to deal with living with HIV. Her life was forever changed. I know that in today's society, living with this sickness doesn't automatically mean a death sentence, but this shouldn't have happened to her. She didn't deserve this. She wasn't the one running around fucking everything in sight. She just loved a man that was a fucking dog.

Right now, I was headed to Jaheim's shop to let him know that we were going to help him set Demario up. I sent him a text making sure he was there, and not to go anywhere. I let him know that I was on my way, and I needed to talk to him. I made it to the shop, and of course, the first person I saw was Brandon. I swear that if this idiot said anything out of his mouth the wrong way, I was gone mace the hell out his ass.

"What's up baby girl? You ready to talk about us now?"

"Brandon, shut the fuck up an go to hell before I mace your dumb ass."

That boy was really special and lacked common sense. I walked in the shop and spoke to Erica, the front desk manager. She was a sweetheart. I walked to the back and knocked on Jaheim's door. I could hear that he was on the phone, so I just waited for him to finish the call before and let me know to come in.

"What's up, lil mama? You look upset."

"I am fucking furious right now."

"What the fuck is wrong, Aaliyah?"

"I want to help you get that motherfucking Demario. I got a plan to help you set that bitch up and his people for fucking good."

"Whoa, lil mama, what are you talking about? What's really good, baby?"

"Chantelle's got HIV. That motherfucker gave my best friend fucking HIV, Jaheim!"

I broke down as I explained to Jaheim the conversation I had with Chantelle last night. I cried because I was hurt for my best friend. She honestly didn't deserve this, and I was furious. I told Jaheim our plan to get Demario to meet us at Chantelle's house and let then take it from there.

"Aaliyah, if you are serious, I will call my nigga Snoop and set that shit up tonight."

"We are serious, Jaheim. The only thing that Chantelle asks is that she pulls the trigger on Demario."

"What, no I can't let her do that, Aaliyah. She is not ready for that."

"I think she is, Jaheim."

"Why do you think she is, Aaliyah?"

"Because her life is ruined. She can never have a family or children. He took that from her, and she doesn't want him to expose any other woman this!"

"Ok, y'all get that nigga to the spot tonight at nine o'clock and be careful. If anything changes, call me ASAP. I mean it, Aaliyah. We only have one chance at this."

"Ok, Jaheim."

I left out of the shop extremely emotional and anxious. I have never set anyone up for anything. Hell, I couldn't even set a date for my own wedding let alone a murder, but this had to be done and done tonight.

I called Chantelle and let her know everything was good. The plan was for her to get Demario to meet her at her spot while Jaheim and his homeboy Snoop would be waiting for him. They needed him to tell who shot Jaheim's cousin, and then it would be up to Chantelle to pull the trigger. They had a spot in the woods where they would take him so that no one could hear the shots. Chantelle was down for it, and so was I. I called out of work and class because I needed to focus on tonight. The plan was to have dinner with Chantelle around seven and have Demario meet us around nine.

***

Around seven, Chantelle sent Demario a text message asking him to please meet her at her house. She told him that she just needed to talk to him about them. Like the sad little puppy, he is he agreed, not knowing he was walking into his own death trap.

"Chantelle, are you ready for this?"

"Aaliyah, nothing will change my mind. I won't allow him to hurt anyone else."

"Ok."

"That's him. Go in the back and text Jaheim. Tell him that Demario is here."

I went into the bedroom and texted Jaheim. I then listened on as Chantelle and Demario talked.

"Chantelle, baby I'm sorry. Those other women don't mean anything to me. Please forgive me. We can get married and have a family. Please, I need you, baby."

"Oh, you need me now. Why do you need me, Mario? Why do you need me but constantly hurt me? How could you need me and find pleasure with other bitches? You don't love me, Mario. You used me. All you did was use me. I only called you over here to let you know that you will never hurt me again or anybody ever again. You will not be able to spread your nasty ass dick around to anyone."

"Chantelle, baby, what are you saying?"

"You gave me fucking HIV you bastard, and yes dumb ass, you have it too! How the fuck could you do this to me? If you wanted to fuck around with nasty ass hoes, why the fuck would you not protect yourself? How could you be so stupid Mario?"

"Are you serious, you have HIV?"

"No dummy, we have HIV. I haven't been with anyone but you. I was the loyal one, and now I have to suffer because of you, but don't worry. You won't suffer for long."

"The fuck you mean?"

"I mean, any second now Jaheim and his homeboy are walking through that door. You seem to have diarrhea of the mouth, and you love to pillow talk. Well, your bitch Star is the cousin to Jaheim's homeboy, and two years ago when you and your people killed that kid on the block Kelton, well that was Jaheim's cousin. Surprise motherfucker, how does it feel to be set up?'

"Chantelle, you fucking trippin' right now, so I'm gone leave before you do something fucked up."

I watched as Demario walked to the door. As soon as he opened the door, he was face to face with the barrel of Jaheim's gun.

"Where the fuck you going, man?" I heard Jaheim ask Demario.

Hearing Jaheim's voice was my cue to come from the back. It was time to end this boy's life, but he brought this shit in himself. Jaheim and Snoop walked Demario to Snoop's Chevy Tahoe and him in. Chantelle and I followed behind in my car. I needed Chantelle to focus cause there was not turning back now. I looked over at my best friend, and she was staring off into space. Her eyes held no emotion, and the look on her face was expressionless.

"Chantelle, you sure you ready for this? I can text Jah and just tell him to do it."

"No Aaliyah, I'm doing this."

We arrived at the spot, and it was too late to turn around. I parked behind Snoop and Jah, and I sat there with Chantelle until we received the text from Jaheim that it was time. After 20 minutes of sitting in the car in silence, the text tone from my phone scared the both us. I looked at my screen, and it was a text from Jah.

Jah: Let Chantelle know we got what we needed. The little bitch sang like a fucking bird. All it took was for me to tell him that I would talk to you and Chantelle and spare his life. Let's do this.

Me: Ok.

"You ready, Chantelle? If you want to back out, let me know now."

"No, let's go."

We all got out of the cars. Jah and Snoop had Demario blindfolded and tied up. I held Chantelle's hand as we walked over to Jaheim.

"Alright Chantelle, all you have to do is aim and pull the trigger. It's three bullets and one in the chamber, so you got four shots. Empty that shit on that motherfucker if you have to."

I listened as Jaheim and Snoop instructed Chantelle on how to aim and shoot.

"Take his blindfold off."

Snoop did as Chantelle asked and took off the blindfold so that Chantelle and Demario were face to face. She pointed the gun directly at Demario.

"Chantelle baby, please don't do this. I am sorry! We can work this out…"

That was the last thing Demario said. Chantelle had shot him four times in the chest. When the last shot hit Demario, Chantelle through the gun down and fell to the ground. I ran over to my best friend and grabbed her. I sat there and let her cry. Jaheim and Snoop left us alone so that she could have her moment. I was hurting for my friend, but I had her no matter what.

Epilogue

Here it was Valentine's night, and I had something special planned for my girl. The night we popped Demario, Aaliyah proved herself as a true rider. After Chantelle killed the fuck nigga, Snoop and I went to his people house, and just like Demario said, they were all there. Snoop and I went in popped all of them and left, no words were said, just straight shots. They didn't even have a chance to pull out and start bussing back. The entire job took three minutes. That's how I did shit, in and fucking out.

Aaliyah help set the entire thing up, and it all went flawlessly. She never once showed fear, and she held Chantelle down the entire time. If she was scared, lil mama was a pro at hiding that shit, and that shit was sexy as fuck to me. My heart went out to Chantelle she had to deal with living with this sickness for the rest of her life. She was maintaining the best she could, and of course, Aaliyah was gone ride with her every step of the way. I let Chantelle know that if there was ever anything she needed not to hesitate to ask. I even put her on my company insurance policy so that she could get the medical coverage she needed. I haven't really heard much from my cousins since I fired Cherie, I really didn't give a fuck either. My aunt and I were still cool, and that's all that mattered. I made sure that my aunt had money every week to take care of Cherie's daughter.

I haven't had a Valentine's Day date in so long that I didn't know where to start. I wanted to plan a nice dinner for Aaliyah with flowers, chocolate, and the whole works. I asked my store managers Erica and Stacey to help me set everything up. I started by having Edible Arrangements delivered to her at her job and her school along with flowers. I had Keith place a teddy bear on the outside of her car when she got off work. I wanted to have her favorite restaurant cater our dinner tonight, so I called City Grill in advance and had her favorites delivered to my house for the night. The most important gift of the night was the diamond necklace with the letter 'J' on it. I was giving it to her tonight.

We were in the beginning stages of our relationship, but I wanted to let her know that I was in it the long way. I was serious about this. The way she held shit down the night Demario got killed let me know that she was the one and would hold me down if shit got bad. I wanted her to wear this necklace so that she knew I was gone

hold her down as well. I sent lil mama a text message letting her know

to meet me at my house at eight. I also cashed app her $500 to go and

buy herself something sexy for the night.

I thanked my managers for all of their help today with getting

everything set up. I always blessed their pocket with a little something

extra for the help. It was already after six, and I needed to be on my

way to the crib. I made it home just as the Uber Eats from City Grill

was pulling up. I let them in a set the food up as I went to the back and

got dressed. I left both Uber drivers a $ 100 tip for their services.

By 7:30, I was dressed and looking damn good. My baby was

due any time, and everything was perfect. Although I'd been sending

her flowers and Edible Arrangements all day, I had some at my spot

waiting for as well. At exactly eight o'clock, my lil mama was walking

up the driveway. She was so fucking sexy in a red off the shoulder

sweater dress that stopped right above the knee. The thigh high sexy

black boots that zipped up on the side were on her feet. She had her

signature curls in her hair, and they were placed perfectly. Her face was beautiful with minimal makeup, but those lips were shining perfectly.

"Damn, lil mama, I said get something sexy, not shut shit down. You are looking so fucking beautiful."

"Thank you, Jaheim, and thank you for all my flowers and gifts today. You really made my day perfect."

"No thanks needed. You deserve it, and your night has just begun. Come on in."

"Jaheim, you did all this for me?"

"I damn sure did, well I really didn't do it. I paid for it all though, and it was my vision. I had my store managers help me with the decorations, and of course, I had City Grill deliver the food, and I remembered your favorite was the grilled chicken salad with onions and peppers with peppercorn parmesan dressing."

"You remembered all that?"

"I remember everything about you lil mama. Why are you so surprised? I listen to you baby girl, and I put everything about you in my mental when it comes to you. Before we eat, I have something for you."

I reached in my pocket and pulled out the Zales Jewelers box that held her necklace.

"Aaliyah Marie James, I want you to wear this necklace to make this shit official. I know that we are in the beginning stages of building our relationship, but I am in this shit for good. I have dealt with so much hurt and pain to the point that my heart was cold. It took you to come in and break the ice. I am giving you this necklace because I want the world to know that you are mine. I know it won't be easy because we both have our own personal demons that we have to deal with, but I am willing to go through this with you, as long as you promise not to give up on me when shit get hard. We gotta talk shit through. Communication is the key, lil mama. So Aaliyah, will you wear this necklace and be my girl."

"Yes, Jaheim Rashawn Martin, I will be your girl. I promise to communicate with you and through everything."

That night I made love to my girl. This relationship would not be easy. We have both had to deal with heartbreak and pain, but it took for us to find each other to realize that we both can love again. It would take time, but I wanted this. I was going to be her biggest supporter in whatever she wanted in life. I was going to love my curvaceous woman. I would love every curve, every stretch mark, and every dimple. I would make sure that she knew how beautiful she was every day, even on the days she didn't feel beautiful herself. Although we were just starting out, I knew that she would one day be my wife and the mother of my children. Getting money and securing our bag was what it was all about. Like they say, *"Roses are red, and my thug love was true…"*

The story of Aaliyah and Jaheim was just beginning.

CPSIA information can be obtained
at www.ICGtesting.com
Printed in the USA
LVHW031814230419
615253LV00002B/278